Secrets Within the Soul

Secrets Within the Soul

TONI JACKSON

ISBN: 978-1-957009-56-8 (sc)

Library of Congress Control Number: 2022916576

To all of the women and men, young and old who thought
there was no one to talk to or nowhere to go.

Trust in the Almighty God in the name of Jesus!

Keep your head up!

Any similar storylines are by total coincidence and are written by the leading of the Holy Spirit. All sentences are based on everyday life.

CONTENTS

Secrets Within the Soul book cover Description

(Front cover)
The woman represents the beauty we possess. The orchids are a semblance of how valuable and precious we are as humans. The flower petals in mid-air represent the beauty being shed because of the Secrets Within the Soul never revealed to anyone. We are valuable, unique in our own ways and that should be celebrated.

(Back cover)
The Hummingbird is a reminder that we should live life to its fullest and to enjoy the simplest pleasures in our lives. It also represents joy, healing, and hope.

The butterfly represents transformation. We all have secrets but once we reach our place of maturing or healing and enlightenment a freedom will be apart of our lives.

Dominique

*I*n the lives of many young ladies and older women, there is a reluctance to trust people they know or meet, especially when dating. These females may have had an absence of a strong male role model to teach them right from wrong in relationships. Therefore, in situations of date rape when it occurs within a friendship, marriage, or long-term relationship it is attributed to their attempt to regain trust in men; unlike the female that had a good male role model.

Moreover, there are occasions when sexual abuse from men becomes a part of some of their lives, and trust for some of them may become inevitably destroyed. In addition, denial could set her on a path of constantly trying to trust men; thinking that not all males could possibly be on the same sadistical path.

This is where The Secrets Within the Soul becomes a part of their lives.

Insomuch as, if you become a part of a sexual assault and you know the male involved, and have accusations of rape brought against him, there is a very high chance that the law will not convict him.

Many women still have not spoken up out of fear and the possible disbelief from family members and the courtroom (judge, jury) if bought to trial. This is because most juries would believe since there was an association by short/long term relationship, that rape is not likely. Somehow, believing the answer was really yes and not no.

Dominique is a female who was striving to achieve that perfect love she had heard about many times from her girlfriends. All alone as a teenager with really no one she felt she could talk to she began reaching out for love from male companions. This seemed that it would be the best remedy for the void she had in her life, the lack of love from a father figure. Little did she know that the cost of love, from a male, would cost her virginity.

Losing her virginity, as a teenager made her feel that there was no danger or harm done especially because her girlfriends spoke so highly of their own personal experiences.

Dominique began her first intimate involvement with a guy named Drozer; it gradually evolved into the loss of her virginity.

Dominique had intercourse with Drozer with just an inkling of an idea of what was going to happen or even how. With the insertion of his manhood it broke her skin (hymen), this entrance into her precious jewels caused her to bleed. When the whole act of intercourse was over Dominique realized that she was bleeding. Because of the lack of communication with her parents she just assumed that her menstrual cycle had started for that particular month. She thought to herself, "good at least I am not pregnant". Without recognizing that it was a sign of losing the most precious gift, God had given her.

At such a high price for love (which is priceless) Dominique began finding out that she was only setting herself up for many pitfalls of hurt. Because of her innocence and naiveness, she found herself in the first of many relationships where her love was the only thing that kept the relationships together. And eventually, everything between them just ceased without warning.

Dominique's future relationships were more emotionally painful than she could ever imagine. The next two relationships which were in succession, she found to be with a sense of caring about her feelings but in all Dominique found out that she was not the only female involved with the guy she was going out with. This was something she had discussed with each of her companions in previous conversations, whether she was the one and only or not! Of course, their response was she was the one and only, with the intent to keep her holding onto something that had no substance or future.

Left alone now, she was more shattered. Confused about what she was really looking for in a relationship Dominique's heart was broken in what seemed to be in more pieces than when she had been torn in the involvement with Drozer.

There was a period in Dominique's life when she felt there was a need to step back and take a look at the downhill emotional roller coaster she was riding. When she did look back at all the wrong moves she had made Dominique felt she could improve the odds of her success in the love game she had been playing, by just simply being tougher within her personality, playing harder to get, and standing firmer in her decision-making with the male factor involved.

Dominique was now content with the decision she made, which by the way was made in a fairly short period, almost as though she was missing out on something. Instead, of healing and maturing she stepped forward into another relationship.

In the span of approximately three years, she met a young gentleman, Andy, who cared for her more than she had seen in past involvements with guys. The one thing she noticed that did not seem to disappear was the fact that he also wanted to have sex with her.

Dominique expressed how she felt about each time she met someone (of the male gender) the subject of having sex never seemed to cease. After talking about it, they both felt her feelings didn't seem to play a major role in the place of sex. Dominique was now forced with the judgment of either standing by her decision or giving in; after all, she was still young. If she settled for not having sex there was a great possibility of losing him. And in letting her guard down would result in not keeping up her standards she had set and a huge chance that the love will be down the drain. Because she stood her ground and continued to say no, she didn't want to grind with him, in an outside wooded area that seemed to be nothing but trouble, he picked up a large stone with sharp rigid edges threatening her. They had been walking casually when he came up with this idea. He said to her, "if you don't cooperate I'm going to smash you with it." Out of fear of dying and still not wanting to lose him, she went along with what he told her to do.

During the whole act of Andy trying to reach his peak of ecstasy Dominique just stood there, leaning against the wall, not going along with what he was doing until he said "Dominique, what's wrong with you? You better act like you know and move your body to make me feel good!" So she proceeded and started moving along. She had no feeling in the act whatsoever. The feeling of love was not present, she felt used, belittled, alone and empty.

Before leaving the vacant lot he briefly kissed her cheek and began walking out. Dominique stood limp against the wall for a few seconds as if to gather her feelings first and then her thoughts as to what had just happened. Then she followed along when Andy called her to come on. She was in a state of a daze.

Little did Dominique know or understand about these occasions she had been experiencing, but she was allowing herself to be conditioned, a psychological terminology, into the fear of losing male companions. Conditioning is a learned behavior of a particular situation that after it has been practiced continuously over a period of time with the same result it appears to the individual to be a normal reaction.

Dominique's relationship continued with Andy but the occasions of him wanting to be outside grinding on her increased to the point of being, outrageously audacious. He would do it at train stops, on the stairwells and behind houses. Dominique, at these times felt as though she was numb, as though her feelings fell asleep while she was standing awake about the whole grinding act.

As time went on, it seemed apparent that Andy would resort to this manner of behavior when he could not figure out where to go to have sex.

Over the years Dominique and Andy were together there were many times where he would call her to come to see him giving her the impression that they would spend quality time together. But much to her surprise the phone call was a sex call. By the time she met up with him he would take her to a place he set up, by way of male friends, to use their place for a period of time, to have sex.

The first time Andy planned this secret sex call caused Dominique to experience that numb feeling which was becoming all too familiar, as if she were just having a normal reaction.

When they arrived at the apartment that Andy had gotten keys for there was no pretense. He took her straight to the bedroom told her to take off her clothes because he did not have much time. She reluctantly stood there with the thought that she didn't know whose bed this was and she was not going to take off her clothes. When Andy saw that she was not going to cooperate he began to take her clothes off himself. Dominique's reaction was one that may as well have been a manikin's because she didn't move, with the exception of Andy moving her arms and legs to get the clothes off and he walked her across the room to the bed leaving the pile of clothes where she stood. He did his business, got up, got dressed and told her to hurry up and get dressed so they could get out of there.

As you can see Dominique's view of how good intimacy should be was becoming very bleak as well as tarnished accompanied by the damaging of her already low self esteem, feeling that she was not worth anything but sex.

Eventually, Dominique decided just to go on about her life and not be bothered anymore with Andy especially after they got into a fight one night because she just out and out didn't budge toward his advancement to have sex.

By this time she had only been spending time with him sporadically so it didn't have a great affect on her.

Sometime went by and Dominique met someone by the name of Drib. She felt he was handsome. They exchanged phone numbers. Dominique felt that maybe she would just add him to the host of phone numbers she had been collecting over some time, numbers which she used from time to time to hold conversation when she was bored. It didn't go that way. They began visiting one another and talking a great deal on the telephone.

Though Dominique's acquaintance with Drib was very short lived it also involved having sex. This association consisted of not only sex but a gun was also comprised; a 44 caliber-automatic, with a 14 bullet clip. He pointed it at her one day to intimidate her into having sex with him. That was not the only time he used it, alongside that he would point it at any given time for whatever bazaar reason he felt. There was a time that just because she was talking to an old acquaintance there was almost a great big shoot out. From this nightmare of what was so innocent she made her mind up that she did not want to be associated with Drib anymore.

A few days had gone by and she expressed to him that she did not want to be bothered anymore, while standing outside of his house. He said it was okay and they walked away from each other. Dominique's girlfriends were nearby and she continued the night on with them. Until Drib decided to go into a neighboring house, going went into the back bedroom and pointed his gun out of the window to shoot at Dominique and whomever she was with. But by the Grace of God's mercy she recognized the gun being slipped out of the window and she and her girlfriends ran for cover behind a truck parked very close by.

For once, in what had been a long time, she had the time and chance to spend with her girlfriends and wouldn't you know it something like this happens.

The personal effects of this relationship between Dominique and Drib had long-term effects upon her. Many of her nights were riddled with dreams of being shot at, being killed or even being shot multiple times, at most the number of bullets she could remember entering her body in the dreams was fourteen, left laying on the floor of someone's house for dead with no one to help her.

Though these dreams happened more often than not she managed to keep her right state of mind. And for the first time in a long time, she had found a friend she could confide in. This was what she believed helped her thru all of those tough spots she had experienced until now.

Her name was Tee. Dominique felt comfortable telling her innermost feelings to Tee. There were often times Dominique would feel that no one cared about her, especially the male gender. She would cry all the time and ask herself what was wrong with her that she had so many problems holding on to or just even being able to capture a good male relationship the way she had seen so many other girls do while growing up. She began to think she was not pretty enough, smart enough and that she would never attain the type of love she had been looking for so long.

Being able to talk to Tee allowed Dominique to have a broader view of why things were not going the way she wanted them to. Tee explained, from her point of view that Dominique should never give her whole heart the way she'd been doing in past relationships. She rationalized that while in a relationship you should keep some of your heart for yourself, for example: "It's okay to give maybe 80 percent of your heart but keep 20 percent for yourself." Dominique began to think and these words seemed to have the remedy of not being hurt so badly after such unions as the one she had in times past. She would soon find out how well this strategy would work.

There was somewhat of joy within Dominique. She knew she had come this far, with the knowledge of sexually transmitted diseases (STD) and she had never experienced this type of trauma. She felt if she had to go thru something such as an STD she would have really lost her mind. But with the peace of mind and absence of STD, she guarded her heart and was willing to try the game of love once again.

In the months of healing, she regrouped her thoughts took the pace, which she thought was slow, and began dating Roger. She decided the best way to go about getting to know him would be to talk on the phone and then graduate to visiting. Everything went well with guarding her heart so she would not be hurt again.

What she did was not allow herself to show any of her feelings or for that matter not even recognize or pay attention to what she really felt. Dominique encamped her heart with what seemed like the highest brick wall surrounded by enclosed steel barriers. This helped her to deal a totally different way concerning her feelings.

She became completely nonchalant toward negative feedback from men and even women. Her way of being kind become nasty. Almost any way that appeared justifiable worked for Dominique as long as she did not get hurt.

She felt she was in a good mode now and well protected. She began visiting Roger and even hanging out with him sometime. The first few times of going over to his house were fun, quiet, and different. And that was all Dominique wanted a friend that would treat her for who she was and not for how much sex he could get out of her. One day Roger bumped into Dominique at the bar so they partied a little bit, and had a drink or two, he then took her by the arm suggesting let's get out of there, with a little hesitation Dominique put on the coat she had been wearing before she came inside the bar, it was cold and snowing outside. She went with Roger not really knowing where he was leading her off-to. They came outside and started walking down the street that's when she realized they were going to his house. She didn't have any fear of what may happen because he had shown her she could trust him. As usual, when they both entered the house they walked straight up to the bedroom this is where

Roger felt most comfortable, it was what he called his dominion. He began resting his clothes, that is to say, taking them off to get comfortable since he was just coming in from work, he turned on the music then he sat on the bed with Dominique leaning over to kiss her, she received him and kissed him back. It seemed like the longer they kissed the deeper the passion was and the more intense the intimacy became. Roger, unlike any of the other times he had spent with Dominique, began to unbutton her blouse and to take off her bra and she exclaimed, "No I don't want to take off my clothes!" but he didn't listen just like all the other times Dominique cried out <u>NO!</u> At that point, she became very serious and began to pull away but because he was such a big guy and she was no more than 140 pounds, there was no getting away. Dominique's body fell limp and despondent by the time he had taken off all of her clothes. Roger proceeded to caress her with his lips over her body and then inserted his manhood into her jewels. He was very what she felt like, very wild with her and it seemed as though it went on for more than 2 hours. After the whole ordeal of sex was over, which she made no action to participate in; he rolled over and fell fast to sleep, not saying one word to Dominique.

She lay opposite him with her back turned to him curled in what looked like a fetal position. She could not believe that this had happened again. It was almost like it was normal and was supposed to happen this way.

While she lay there awake and alone she was angry more than anything and she felt used. And what made it even worst lying awake, was the music that had been turned on, that had rhythm and beat, seemed to now fit the mood to what had occurred, it sounded like Avant Guarde, but as it went on it sounded like a nightmare, just like she was in.

The game Dominique played in shielding her heart worked for the most part when she was with Roger. Though he had sex with her without her consent she lay opposite him under the sheets, as if her feelings didn't matter, and ignored all her negative feelings toward Roger. She continued to express to Roger that she wanted their relationship to be more than visiting each other and in the finale having sex. He went along with her wishes for weeks at a time. One Friday evening Dominique stopped by to see Roger he was spending a quiet evening watching television, and he was very surprised to see her when he answered the door. When Dominique came in he received her with a warm welcome. They talked for hours, held one another, and even gave each other a few intimate kisses. Before they knew it was about 4:30, 5:00 a.m. Without any hint of what was going to happen next, Roger lost control of being a good gentleman and began taking off Dominique's pants. Once again she was fighting to keep her clothes on. She lost the battle of keeping her sexuality to herself with his insertion. Roger knew she was not on any type of birth control so within the two minutes the act lasted, at the peak of his pleasure; he did what he called a quick draw to assure that she would not get pregnant.

Dominique rolled over this time and a tear fell from her eye but right at this moment, she knew she was pregnant. Little did she know that it was Jesus letting her know what was to come in the near future.

At that time while Dominique was now, in what seemed to be a normal position, a fetal position, Roger had gotten up and hurried along, to get ready for work, and to take Dominique home, in order for him to get to work on time.

For about a month and a half, Dominique didn't call or see Roger. During that time she went for her check-up with the gynecologist. She had been counting the days since her last period and by this time it was up to 46 days since her last cycle began. The test that had been taken to see if she was pregnant was positive at 6 weeks. This was not really a surprise to Dominique especially because she had heard God's voice that morning after the incident with Roger, telling her beforehand she was pregnant (she heard his voice not even being saved from her sins).

She knew now she had to tell Roger. They made arrangements to see each other on a Saturday night with him not knowing her agenda. That night came and when Dominique told him he didn't want to receive what she had told him about her pregnancy. He talked to her and expressed how he really felt, of course, he was angry and in a state of denial: He explained, "that he would get in touch with her to give his final decision," as to whether he wanted to go along with her pregnancy, which as it turned out, he didn't want to go through it. The night Roger called to give Dominique his answer of no made her feel as though her feet had fallen from underneath her. After she hung up the phone she began to cry, she then called Tee telling her to come to meet her she needed someone she could talk to. By the time she got halfway around the corner, Tee had already run to meet her knowing that something was terribly wrong. She immediately gave her a hug and Dominique really began to cry sorely, giving all the details as to what had just happened with Roger. She explained tearfully, "Roger no longer wants to be bothered with me and he actually said, not to call him or if I see him on the street not to speak to him." This hurt more than anything she could imagine. Mostly, because Dominique never wanted any children from the beginning and she felt if she did ever get pregnant she did not want to do it all alone, she found herself right in the middle of what she never wanted to happen. After that night Roger saw her about 1 to 2 times more within 3 years. To make things even worst she found out she was carrying triples, two girls and a boy. This broke Dominique emotionally, she was depressed, confused, and all alone and did not knowing what she should do, so she prayed about it, asking Jesus to show her what to do with the babies. Whether she should get rid of them, by way of abortion or adoption, the answer came out to be, to keep them.

The constant looking for love never ceased. But one thing Dominique began to see and know was that she was raised in a Christian atmosphere and in growing up she stayed in church and it was now time to start heading back that way. Because that would be the only _real_ love she would ever know in her life. Besides that, she was reminded that there should be only one covenant made and that's with the one you marry. Every time you lay to have sex you bring the Lord into that covenant and that's not what was ordained to be.

Although she knew this she met someone else and this experience was unlike all the rest, without usury. His name was Ken and he loved her and treated her with respect but in the end, he could not accept that he was falling in love and left without warning.

Dominique always believed that God wanted her to see that not everyone was out to use her and that was why Ken came into her life.

After that point Dominique got saved, becoming a born-again Christian, and realized that the love she had been looking for all along was standing right there waiting to be accepted into her heart His name is ***JESUS.***

Susan got married to her husband Victor at 25 yo. The relationship between Susan and Victor could not have been any better than it was in the first two years of their marriage where there was caring, gentleness, and kindness this gradually turned into situations of carelessness towards Susan. Victor began to come behind her to snatch her by her hair to kiss her whenever he got the urge to kiss her. The kisses were cold without any emotion, and abrupt. Totally unusual from what she had become accustomed to.

Susan didn't quite understand why Victor had initiated such behavior, especially because it was nothing he had done before, even during their courtship. She supposed that his work had become stressful and this was his outlet.

Weeks went by and Victor's aggressiveness escalated into snatching her clothes off, anywhere in the house, and having sex with her vigorously. Until she was so stiff and in so much pain that he could not reach his peak of ecstasy. Her inner legs became badly bruised. The entrance to her jewels swelled to the point that it had closed up and had to be packed with ice. Tears of shock and hurt poured from Susan's eyes but Victor didn't appear to have any remorse at all for her.

Susan was afraid, depressed, and felt hopeless. She knew that she didn't have anyone she felt she could talk to. Particularly, because Victor had threatened her not to tell anyone because it would be worse the next time.

She figured out that some of this behavior was attributed to the sudden pressures and demands placed upon him in the workplace.

Now Susan knew if she did go to talk with her father and or her brothers she would lose her husband, due to death. Susan felt as though her world had crumbled all around her and there was no firm foundation. Either she could stay with Victor and hope his instability would sustain to normal levels of caring or leave which would indicate to her father and brothers something was definitely wrong, then she would have to really hope they didn't hurt him in any way.

As time went by, approximately 1 to 2 weeks, Susan thought earnestly over her situation. During that time Victor came home one-night drunk, she knew that he had been out drinking, at this point Susan feared for her life. She didn't know what to do so she hurried along, turned off the lights, got into the bed, and pretended as if she were asleep for a long period of time before Victor made it up the stairs to their master bedroom. He noticed that her head was buried under the covers therefore he went into the master bathroom to remove the stench of alcohol from his body.

Susan lay there in bed, under the many blankets, because winter had not broken yet, and gave a sigh of relief. Her thoughts were, "he's not going to bother me! He's too drunk to do anything straight let alone have sex".

Much to her surprise the shower he had taken invigorated and stimulated him more than she had hoped. And in his mind, he was capable of doing anything just as if he had not gotten drunk. He climbed into their king-size bed, moved over until he reached Susan on the other side, and began to kiss her until it hurt. If that wasn't enough he began to bite her neck, not small and loving nibbles but large harsh bites that left teeth marks on her neck. The process continued, instead of unbuttoning her nightgown he ripped it open and fondled her bosom with his mouth until they began to tear. Then the inevitable occurred he did things with his mouth he had never done before, he then entered her with his vigorous acts as he had done in the recent past.

Just as anyone that has been conditioned to an activity or behavior Susan was no different in her response to what was being done to her. She was motionless, had no sentiment, even though this was her husband, she stared out into what seemed like space hoping it would be over very soon.

Unlike Dominique, Susan did not cry out to God as her Lord and Savior Jesus Christ, she carried this load all by herself. Susan's ***secret was very hidden,*** only Victor, Susan, and Jesus knew about it, to whom she didn't know she could look up to heaven and cast all her cares upon him for he cares for her (1 Peter 5:7) KJV.

*　*　*

On the night before Dominique decided to give her life to Christ, it was almost like any other night with the exception of going out with her girlfriend to a nightclub. They danced, mingled a little with the crowd, ate, and drank. This was something Dominique felt she owed to herself.

Though the music played loudly it was yet a calm and quiet atmosphere. Before she realized it, it was closing time for the club, 2 a.m. She was a good distance from home but it didn't matter this night because she had gotten a rent-a-car for the weekend. This enabled her to get home fairly quick and safely, even though she had two lightweight drinks. Her girlfriend drove also and they went their separate ways.

Once Dominique arrived home she realized that she had made plans with her family members to go to church service the next morning, which was Sunday.

When she got up on Sunday she made further arrangements as to how she would meet up with everyone that was going. The decision was her family would ride together and Dominique would drive the car she had. This was best, she could then leave at her own convenience going and coming back. Especially because they were leaving from a different location, about 20 minutes from where she was. It was settled she would meet everyone at the church.

When Dominique arrived, upon entering the church, the music that was being played was that of a different beat than she had been listening to the night before and for that matter the past years of her life. She found a seat and instead of getting right into the service she kept looking at the door each time someone came in, hoping her family would be there very soon because this was only her second time there and she didn't know anyone in this large place.

Eventually, she stopped paying attention to the door. Then the minister of the hour made an altar call. With everything in Dominique's natural power she was going to stay right in the seat, she had found. Without any thought she got up out of her seat and walked to the front of the church for the altar call, this was for anyone that didn't know Jesus as his or her personal Lord and Savior. While standing there two other people came up too. The minister continued to speak as the Holy Spirit of the Lord lead him to do so. He then walked from the pulpit to talk to Dominique and spoke as the Lord told him to tell her, "don't leave here today without accepting Jesus into your heart because it may be your last chance." Then the Elders of the church took Dominique and those who chose to change the ways of life for Christ back into a room, in another area of the church. The Elders (these are the leaders of the church that are directly under the

Pastor) spoke to them concerning salvation, deliverance from sins, and accepting Jesus into their hearts. It was a matter of letting Jesus know all of the sins they had committed up until this point and that they wanted to give him all of their sins and hurts for the promise of life eternal with Jesus. Dominique thought to herself WOW! Is that all? Is it that easy? Here's a man that I can get very intimate within the spirit and in truth and he won't hurt me, take advantage of me, abuse me, lie or use me as a piece of meat that could be used as a sex object, she felt this was the greatest thing of all, so she went for it.

The Elders of the church then took them back into the sanctuary as new children in Christ. Then the doors of the church were opened, that is to say, if they didn't have a church they belong to as members they were welcome to join this branch of Zion.

Dominique began to cry without understanding why she was crying. The tears rolled and rolled from her eyes continually and she could not stop them.

She and the other two people all joined as members. At that point, the whole congregation was invited to make a line and welcome their new converts/ members.

She felt this was wonderful everyone that came around to the front of the sanctuary either shook her hand or gave her a hug, something she didn't have in a very long time from anyone. She cried even harder, the tears didn't seem to want to stop.

At the dismissal of church service, Dominique said, "Goodbye" to those she had met while she was there. Her family never showed up.

While she drove away in the rent-a-car, a white 1991 Cougar with 4 doors, she never dreamed it would lead her to take this direction in life. She thought about all that was said and done. In pursuit of driving the car, it felt like a feather going about in the direction she instructed it to go. She also realized that the feelings she had felt much of her teenage years, now in her mid20, up until that day were the weights of the world she never dismissed or discharged by reason of not telling anyone all of the things she was going through back then. Now Dominique had given them to Jesus and felt 100 percent better. The tears played in a great deal of her cleansing, from all of her scared emotions.

Dominique didn't talk to anyone about her good news for about a week then she broke her silence.

She became more humble, kinder, and patient, and learned how to treat people better. A few of the many ways of Christ she allowed herself to be conformed to at this point.

One of the more challenging things for Dominique was learning not to have male companions as she had in the past. After about 8 years she felt she was strong enough in her spirit man to have a male she could talk to.

Dominique did meet someone his name was Morton. Their friendship started off with long conversations. One night Morton saw Dominique while he was driving down the street, he stopped, talked with her for a while then they both noticed how late it had gotten. They were talking for about an hour and a half. He then asked her would she mind if he took her home, she felt comfortable with his presence so she said, "yes". Since she was on the porch visiting a classmate from college she had to go into the house to say goodbye, and also to collect her belongings.

Dominique was now on her way home and was somewhat happy she didn't have to call a cab.

Upon Dominique arriving home, their conversation continued as if she had not reached her destination. Once Morton noticed he was sitting there idol just listening then responding, he pulled out of the parking spot he had driven into, with her permission, proceeding to drive until he came to a very scenic, serene place surrounded by pretty flowers, and a lake with the moon shining on it allowing the night to take its course because it was such a nice summer night. They both began to realize that they were hungry so Morton said, "come on I know a place that stays open all night." So they went to get something to eat. By this time Dominique felt the time really was getting too late, it was 2:30 a.m. She told him to take her home because this was now really out of her normal limits of being out. He respected her wishes and proceeded in the direction to take her home. This made Dominique happy because he seemed to pay attention to her wishes. On the way to her house, he made a statement that he needed to stop home for a minute but he would take her home as soon as he ran into his house and came right out. This was okay to Dominique because he doubled parked and left her in the car with it on. It took all of 5 minutes which was a relief to her.

She finally arrived home. At that point, she began to get out of the car and he asked her could he come in. That question made her slow her pace for a few seconds to think about what he was exactly asking. Given their time spent together and his commitment to showing her his respect she said, "okay", without any second thoughts. They both entered the quiet house, which was minus Dominique's triples, who were now away in their 1st year/semester of college. She offered him a seat in the living room while she got situated in put her belongings away, she turned on the gospel music before leaving the room just to remind him of the kind of girl she was.

Dominique now re-entered the living room continuing their talking. The only difference was he started to kiss her in her mouth. Dominique thought to herself, "This is nasty; I don't know him like that." So she began to verbally express herself, asking him what was wrong with him, did he lose a section of his brain or something, and why was he acting like this, especially because he tried to force her mouth open by squeezing her jaws with his fingers. That didn't stop him. Her eyes got very large as if she were in shock and she began to fight Morton to get him to stop, but that just seemed to fuel the moment of his so-called passion. His mode escalated to turning off the lamp that sat adjacent to the sofa, applying more force to getting Dominique to move and to cooperate with him moving into the middle of the living floor away from any objects she may have been able to club him with. He went straight into action not stopping for one moment even in the process of pulling her clothes from her body. He held her arms with one hand and used the other hand to take her clothes off, bottom only. He did things dazzling to her then he decided to penetrate as a man would into her jewels. Dominique lay there not wanting to believe this was happening, so she blocked it out of her emotions so she would not feel any hurt. This is what allowed her to stay friendly with Morton. What she didn't realize she allowed some of her old habits back into her heart and her life, the act of conditioning. Which comes under the category of mind control. That very next day she allowed him to take her out to brunch, paying no attention to the reality of the whole situation. This permitted their relationship to continue on. She began missing lots of church services.

Dominique began to see things for what they really were after a short period of time, this was not right and she realized she was sinning all over. She had to let Morton know it was over between them and their relationship had to cease. It was at this space in time that she noticed her focus was altered. She also explained to him, even though he was very familiar with how her Christian walk should be, although he was not active in his own Christian walk. (Amos 3:3 KJV: "How can two walk together unless they both be agreed"). This verse made it easy to proceed in her walk alone.

She started attending services, reading her bible, and praying the way she should. These things are essential in the Christian walk and she could not set them aside in order to do what she used to do, because, she would find herself in the same predicament. She also had to go thru deliverance from all those evil things she allowed back into her life. Dominique's life was much better once she let go of her heavy load; Letting Jesus carries it, not her. But one thing was still against her, Morton was trying very hard not to let go of the relationship with Dominique.

It was approximately 3 months and Morton stopped by out of the blue, right before she was leaving to go out. It was daytime; the sun was shining brightly through the open blind at the window and in spite of that it didn't stop Morton from trying to take off Dominique's panties from under her jean skirt. This started without any warning just, BAM! Dominique held on to her panties and her skirt with everything in her being. Pushing him, tying her legs together, everything she could think of, while up against the living room wall for support, in her fight for victory. It didn't work. He pinned her down with his hands and his weight to the floor once he got her away from the wall leaving marks on the white wall. Once he got her panties off he began to razzle her.

Morton never even thought for one moment about the window being a witness to his harsh act.

The whole act was over and Dominique was steaming MAD. She got herself together to go out while he sat on the sofa. When she returned to the living room she turned on the music so loud she could not hear Morton talking to her. This allowed all of Dominique's frustration and anger to vent without snapping or hurting him in any way. He got angry and left, which was good for Dominique because she was ready to go anyway.

Later that night after she went shopping she went to prayer service and when she started praying she began to cry not letting anyone around her to see her emotion or even know what was wrong for those who saw the tears. These tears she realized were okay to cry because it was the beginning of another cleansing process.

Dominique was very determined to get on the right track. She continued to take all of the necessary steps that would strengthen her walk in Christ.

After about 9 months of the worse that could ever happen to Dominique happened. Morton stopped by as he had in the past months to talk so she answered the door. She had been sleeping, it was the early, early hours of that Sunday morning in June and Dominique thought nothing of it because it was something he had done many times before. Mostly when something was on his mind and he wanted someone to talk to he felt comfortable with. She sat on the sofa in a knot, hoping he would be finished talking very soon, since she had to go to work in a few hours. It was almost like an instant replay from the very first time she allowed him into her place, he raped her again. The only difference this time was she prayed vehemently against him because she realized Jesus was on her side and Dominique on his, unlike before, now she was complete.

The only problem with that was though she prayed she was outside of the will of God: she never should have let him in regardless of the situation. Which means, as long as she was walking and moving in the parameters of the Holy Spirit no evil could touch her, (Psalms 91) KJV: as soon as you get into your own way of seeing and doing things, bad things can happen to you similar to Dominique.

*   *   *

In the following hours, which were about 4 hours, Dominique went to work without any emotion all day long. Directly after work she decided to catch the ending part of Sunday afternoon church service. Within minutes of her entering the door, the minister of the hour began to let the Holy Spirit minister through him, to Dominique. Without him knowing what had happened in the earlier part of the day he called her up to the pulpit speaking directly to her saying "Thus saith the Lord, you are somebody worth waiting for, you are not A PIECE OF MEAT out for the slaughter at will" (this was encouragement that Dominique needed to stay on track.) See, the devil had a trap of destruction that she may not reach her potential in Christ. Dominique cried even as he prophesied to her, still not telling him what had happened. Once she started crying the tears just rolled from her eyes, she allowed them to do so not caring who saw her crying. The only thing was that there were so many tears backed up inside of her it was only a few times, for a few minutes, that she stopped crying after that. Many tried to cheer her up but couldn't, the tears just kept coming down her face. Her Pastor offered to take her home but she didn't even trust him ***that day.*** On the way home on the bus, she prayed the whole way for her tears to stay inside until she got in the door. Low and behold that's how it happened. Once she got in the door at the early hour of about 8:00 p.m. she got ready for bed, got in it, curled up in a fetal position, cried, and sobbed until she fell asleep.

The path of total healing had to start for Dominique just as for anyone else who has been through any type of trauma such as RAPE. Dominique wrote Morton a letter that same week he raped her. The situation, this time was more devastating than any of the other times she was raped. That was one of the reasons she decided to write him to tell of her pain and anger. She knew if he knew who the letter was from he may have not read it. So she wrote in such a way that he had to read almost the entire letter before knowing who had written the letter.

From that day forward whenever Dominique's male acquaintances stopped by for even just a few minutes, coming inside (married or unmarried) she felt nervous and scared but she didn't allow her emotions to show. Most times she knew if they would be stopping by while in the vicinity of her house. But before they got there that was when she got a nervous stomach and sometimes a headache.

She realized that this was a tough road of healing she had to go through but she was willing to go through it.

Dominique also recognized that she was going to have to learn to love and how to be loved unconditionally, with Jesus' AGAPE love, and this would be the road to recovery. In doing this it was about trusting God. Because if she didn't she knew that it would never work trying to do it all by herself.

Jayna a 27 yo. woman who really loved the Lord Jesus and was sold out (submissive) to do his will. There was one weakness though, as with some Christians until they are delivered from those things of the flesh, she allowed herself to have a male acquaintance that was strictly platonic. You may think to yourself that's okay as long as it stays that way. The fact is when you're totally sold out for Jesus your interest should be in him until he sends the man he (Jesus) has picked out for you. Therefore, Jayna was outside of the will of God.

As with Dominique, Jayna also lacked love in her younger years. As Jayna had done up until the day she got saved, she kept a male friend on the side for various worldly reasons. Her exception now was she was not willing to deal with men the way she did when she was not saved.

The friend that Jayna had now his name, Mark. Jayna liked being around him most, though he was not saved, besides her girlfriends at times.

Jayna allowed herself to fall in love with Mark. This happened rather easily because Mark was a real gentleman, easy to get along with, conversations never had any type of arguing, even in disagreements it didn't get out of the way, and most of all he always, always, treated her with the utmost respect. All of this was quite mind-blowing to Jayna.

As their relationship grew they learned more and more about one another. Moreover, their agreement about not having sex still remained in tack.

Mark loved Jayna as much as she loved him. He often would come over with dozens of roses, red and white, or just some nice clothes he felt she would look lovely in.

About a year passed by and Jayna still went to praise and worship service. She worshipped the Lord regardless of her outside relationship with Mark. You should know that this is very dangerous because she was treading on Satan's ground. Jayna and Mark bought a home together; of course, the two of them had separate bedrooms. Gradually, their relationship grew even stronger but there was one area of Mark's life Jayna was concerned about, his soul. Though he frequented church services his soul had not been saved yet. (He had not willingly given up his will to Jesus to become saved.) This was hard for Jayna because Mark had already started talking about marrying her so they could live together as husband and wife; not as roommates.

One day when Jayna came home from work she noticed the dining room table was set for dinner, for two, with candlelight, roses, and orchids. This was not something terribly out of the ordinary because whenever Mark felt extraordinarily loving he would do this. Once he heard Jayna enter the room he came out of the kitchen to greet her with his normal kiss and hug. Dinner was completely done when she came in. He first sat her down at the well-set table, linen table cloth, china, etcetera, and then he told her to close her eyes to receive the 1st portion of their dinner, to her surprise, he served caviar. Secondly, he served filet mignon and russet potatoes with sautéed vegetables. To drink he served sparkling cider. Lastly, was the biggest surprise of all for dessert, he told her to close her eyes again, and when she opened them there was a 2carat diamond and sapphire ring on the plate on top of a plain piece of cheesecake. Mark then proceeded to kneel on the floor by her dinner chair and he formally asked her to marry him. Her emotions were mixed because she loved him so much but he had yet to give his whole heart to Jesus but she still said YES! With this thought in mind and the answer she gave him she was still elated by the event but a little sad because she knew if he didn't get saved while they were engaged she would have to call it off.

For the first 2 months of their engagement, nothing new seemed to be happening. But in the middle of the third month, Mark came to the church's anniversary, where Jayna attended. She was pleased with his decision. Service was really under the anointing power of Jesus that Tuesday night.

And Mark really seemed to be enjoying himself. All of a sudden it became very obvious how much he was enjoying himself. When the power of God fell upon him and he really let go of what he felt he knew he allowed Jesus to come completely into his heart. This was what Jayna had been praying for all along that he would let go and let Jesus totally in. Jayna was wholistically ecstatic. She knew that at this point she could marry Mark as she had hoped all along.

Nine months later Mark and Jayna were married in a large church nearby their home, with all of their family and friends looking on.

Mark remained very loving toward his new wife for all about nine months of their marriage.

Eighteen months were now entirely gone and where Mark appeared to have gotten saved thoroughly was now rapidly fading away. How many know this was a trick of deception? To try to lure Jayna away from her walk-in Christ, because he knew how much she loved him. (He was being used by Satan and didn't even recognize it).

This began with him being rude to Jayna unlike any of the whole relationships they were together. His attendance at church services went from every service to no services at all. He didn't even pray and said so. When she would come home from work she would find him lying around drinking beer and smoking cigarettes. Something he didn't do before. Most of all when they came together as husband and wife, no longer was it loving and pleasurable for Jayna, for the simple reason of Mark always manipulating her. Mentally, physically and emotionally he had a way of making her feel inadequate (saying she was not able to perform her duties as a wife should with her husband) 1 Cor. Chap 7 KJV. Jayna thought to herself, this is a form of rape no matter if he's my husband or not. She also reflected back on how happy she was because Mark had gotten saved. But what she realized most now at this point was that Mark was what she had been praying for but not what Jesus had planned for her life. So it was a matter of dealing with the abuse or just turning her life completely back into Jesus' hands the way it should have been from the beginning. Believing if this was meant to be Jesus would make a way out of no way, seeing to it that Mark would serve Jesus wholly for the rest of his life. Whatever she did she knew she could not divorce him because the Bible clearly states that it's the wrong thing to do. (Matthew 19: 3 – 12, 1 Corinthians 7 : 2 – 14, Matt 5: 31 – 32) KJV.

She fully knew that she was outside of the will of God now. Jayna had allowed her feelings for Mark to camouflage what was really ordained for her life.

Determination what does it mean? It's having a spirit that doesn't give up, resilience, striving, no one or nothing can stand in your way, its just KNOWING that you can do all thing thru Christ who strengthens you.

Attitude in a positive way played a serious part in her life. Dominique knew that the Lord had great things for her life and they had to be accomplished regardless of what obstacles stood in her way. Many times Satan would try to place men in Dominique's life to hinder her in the path that Christ had laid before her. And the choice was totally up to Dominique because Jesus allows us to make our own decisions.

And there was always a constant battle to get rid of the fear of ever being hurt again. To the extent that she knew Jesus would never hurt or harm her in any way but she struggled to give her whole heart to him, that he could move wholistically and miraculously in and thru her, this was her greatest battle. This meant having her will destroyed via Jesus. (Praying with her sincere heart that the spiritual blood clots from all the hurts would be destroyed by the way of his supernatural clot buster, the blood of Jesus, so she would be able to feel his AGAPE love flow through her with his warmth and embrace of love.)

She had to take to heart the word of God that says, "Perfect love (Jesus) casts away all fears" (1 John 4: 18 – 19) KJV and to know that with everything in her that Jesus is her best friend and she his.

She came to recognize the drawbacks where from previous experience, which accounted for the hindrances in her ministry: cowardice, sensitivity, and caring what people thought, some of this stemmed from the rapes she experienced. Understanding this was a hindrance, she also worked on destroying the very manner of it, by the power of the Holy Spirit, through fasting and praying against it.

Her game plan was to continue to repent, renounce, rebuke, and release the Power of God that lived within her, continue in prayer, keep communicating with Jesus and read the word of God consistently.

In knowing what she had to do, she kept pressing forward to a positive road of recovery (that was no more than allowing Jesus to deliver her completely from any residue of hurts or memories.)

She knew this was a must to have VICTORY thru Jesus Christ.

Resilience played a big part in people laughing at her mishaps. She took them as a stepping-stone towards greater accomplishments/victories. She also realized that all the times she experiences that numbness was a defense that allowed her to keep her right state of mind. It was Jesus.

Though it may seem like Dominique, for a long time, could not see the real deal about men, Jesus allowed these things to be that they would glorify his name thru this story.

One good thing that happened in Dominique's life is that through Bible study over the years she learned to trust no man but only to trust Jesus because he will never leave you or forsake you. (Psalms 27, Hebrews 13:5, Psalms 37:25) KJV. Also, that self-esteem is no more than the prideful way that will lead you to fall and will never allow you to give your whole heart to Jesus. In the event you find yourself giving your whole heart to a man it's a form of worship and a big setup from Satan to cause you to fall into the pit of no return. Not being able to go forth in Jesus whole-heartedly, because of it, to tell the whole world how much Jesus loves you and how he's set you free as he did for Dominique.

Dominique and Jayna found out that if you place or allow yourself to be around positive saved people who don't mind encouraging you to do well in the Lord and everyday life you can go very far in your walk for Jesus, knowing that Heaven is your reward.

They both knew that forgiveness had to take place in their deliverance.

They also realized the reality of always learning to give love and then the individual in some manner was no longer in their life. Whether it was family members dying, changing jobs, Bon voyages or just being in a temporary setting, becoming comfortable around those people, and then it was time to depart and no longer be around them. Mostly, it was Dominique who could never understand why she always cried when people came in and out of her life. But one day she realized it was because she was still reaching out for love from people.

As she continues on today it is hard not to reach out to people to love them even though they don't always reach back to love her. Her comfort comes when she mediates on the fact that Jesus loves her and not to be concerned about whether people love or care for her.

For Jayna, it was a little easier to adjust her emotions.

The devil comes to rape you of your walk-in Christ. Physically, emotionally and spiritually. Even before you find out that Jesus is waiting for you with open arms, to love you. At any time you are violated physically or emotionally that is a form of rape. Rape is an act of seizing and carrying away by force; he (the devil; Satan) can't act or respond intelligently, therefore, he uses one of the oldest acts to destroy you. In the physical, as already mentioned, on many occasions, rape is sex taken by force without consent.

In the case of, mostly on Jayna's account and some on Dominique's even if you're saved from your sins rape can happen to you if you aren't in the will of the Lord.

It's a matter of just asking Jesus to come into your heart to forgive you of all your sins, as mentioned with Dominique, then just keeping a real relationship with Jesus so that you will know what his will is for your life. By way of prayer and waiting for the answers from him, before going on your way.

Sometimes, depending on the person they may reach out many times for love at a very high price. So you must stay in the will of God.

Hindrances become a part of that price. For certain individuals thinking little of yourself will cause you to continue to allow the same act to happen over and over. And you may even begin to feel others are better than you because you allowed the enemy to lead you in a way that appears to have complete truth, walking outside of the will of God, causing your soundness to become destroyed. It all depends on how much you have allowed yourself to be trapped in this wicked game. You simply have been blinded to what has really been going on. What? A **stronghold** has taken place in your life even as it was for Dominique thus the fasting and praying had to take place. The battle really is on at this point because Satan then believes he had you but you have to keep up the fight in the spirit and he will no longer have a hold on you, no matter how many ways he comes back at you to defeat you your purpose in Christ.

Dominique's experience of having said No so many times put her on a road she would not have ever imagined. All she could keep in her mind is <u>No</u> means <u>No</u> from the bottom of her heart, whether he forced himself on her or not, but more often than not.

Susan did not find Jesus as her Savior and comforter so that she may become saved, delivered, and set free from all of her hurts, disappointments, pain, and uncertainties.

Trixie

*U*nlike date rape, sex trafficking is another means of undermining individuals. Whether it occurs by being unknowingly lured or sold, it is a heinous crime that takes advantage of the most vulnerable of victims, whether by circumstance or with the use of emotional and physical intimidation and abuse.

Many victims find their lives turned upside down from an early age, with most victims being between the ages of 11-14 years old[1]. Throughout the world, these young victims have a hard time breaking free of the nightmare of their circumstances due to many trafficking situations being family enforced.

Some children are stolen off the streets or from birthday parties, shopping malls and beaches. These children are forced into a heinous life by strangers, and usually never see their families again.

Why would a family involve themselves in trafficking their youngest and most innocent members? There are many reasons, from greed and profitability, to the need for control and punishment by stripping away one's dignity and value.

Some families do not have to resources to provide for all the members, so they make the decision to sell their children in order to be able to keep feeding the ones left behind. Some family members simply like the money they can make from involving children in trafficking, though money is usually a motivating factor.

Two young girls from a poor family go to bed hungry one night, both of them feeling extraordinarily sleepy after drinking some juice their mother made for them. They wake up the next morning in a strange room with a strange man.

The youngest, Eliza, can't stop crying. She is six. The oldest, Mirabelle, is frightened but doesn't show it. She's trying to be brave for her sister. She is eleven.

The likelihood of them ever seeing their families again is slim to none, and as the man forces them to undress at knifepoint, they realize their nightmare has only just begun.

They are inspected and cleaned, their hair is cut and dyed and they are quickly separated in order to keep them compliant. Mirabelle never sees her sister again.

They are swept into a dangerous world of drugs and sex, both of which they know nothing about. Both of which control their every waking moment for the next nine years.

Once these young girls find themselves under the control of a pimp, it's nearly impossible to break free, as they are held in seclusion or with debt over their heads that must be repaid.

The girls are both told they must work until their family's debt is paid in order to see each other again, though no such debt actually exists. The amount changes daily, as the pimp charges them for the food they eat and the bed they sleep in despite neither of them asking to be there.

These victims are made to service several men daily without a moment's break, damaging them both physically and psychologically in ways that can only be helped with deep therapy and professional care if they are ever lucky enough to escape.

They turn to drugs and alcohol, self-harm, and risky behavior in an effort to cope with the life they are forced to live.

At the young age of ten, Eliza already drinks half a pint of hard liquor a day in order to cope. A gift from her pimp, he realized that she's more compliant the drunker she is.

She is made to do things no child should ever have to do, and she has lost all hope for escape after four long years of being passed around dozens of men a day.

Mirabelle is already fifteen and is lying on a cot in a makeshift hospital while a man is cutting the unborn child from her womb.

This is her third abortion. Her pimp doesn't want her to have any responsibilities beyond servicing clients. Mirabelle's drug of choice is heroin, and the tracks up and down her arm earn her a beating for looking unpresentable.

The pimps will use the girls until they no longer see value in them when they either age out of their clientele's tastes or become so damaged by the life that they no longer bring in enough money to be worth it.

Eliza, still relatively young, is being sent to service more and more dangerous clientele. The price is good for the pimp, but for Eliza, the scars both physical and mental will never heal. She plots to escape, but beyond the act of actually leaving, she knows she no longer has anywhere to go.

Her mother sold her into this life, and if she returned, she'd likely sell her again.

Still, the victims like Eliza may try to escape long before then, and it's a battle for them that is hard won if they succeed in getting away at all. The pimps make sure that the victims have nowhere to go or no one to turn to, cutting off all ties from family and friends from the moment they have the victim in their grasp.

Many of those who do escape cannot risk returning to the same families that sold them into trafficking, to begin with, leaving them with few options. Some may return to their pimps out of fear of starvation or a worse life on the streets alone.

She tries to escape one night but is ratted out by a fellow victim who thinks she can win favor with their pimp. She isn't a bad person, but she has learned to take advantage of every opportunity that may find her.

She screams for the pimp to find her soon after she takes off into the deep forest, but the dogs find her easily, nipping at her heels and keeping her in place until she can be brought back to whatever dingy motel they were currently set up in.

Her pimp was angrier that he had ever seen him. He began to beat her, hoping to teach her a lesson, but he didn't stop until she wasn't moving any longer.

Many of those who try to escape end up dead, like Eliza, who was murdered by her kidnapper in a fit of rage at the age of eleven and dumped in a trash heap never to be missed or heard from again.

Mirabelle was finally released by her captors at the age of twenty, but by then her life had been so damaged that she faced an uphill battle of recovery in order to live a normal life.

Children in foster care are especially vulnerable, as they usually have to depend on the love and kindness of strangers in order to survive.

Foster children may become victims of trafficking due to a boyfriend/ girlfriend turned pimp who gains their trust and love before they begin to invite others to become involved with the victim as well, usually against their will or through coercion or guilt.

Traffickers find a way to isolate their victims further by making them feel as if no one loves them. They tell the children that "No one is coming back for you," or that "They allowed you to end up in here," in order to break their morale and force them to depend on the trafficker.

Sometimes they use threats and violence to get what they want, but other times they make the victim feel loved in order to guilt them into doing what they desire.

Foster children are also in danger of being groomed by those with authority over them with the offer of new clothes or food they may never have experienced before, the offer of safety or stability, and other gifts that might be used to entice the child to engage in inappropriate behavior.

These types of pimps are even more dangerous than strangers, as they have a personal connection to the victim that they use to their advantage in order to force them to feel like they must repay a debt. They may force the victims to sell drugs and then use that to threaten them. They may be physically or verbally abusive. They may even threaten other siblings in close proximity to the victim in or to get them to comply.

Signs to look out for in children that may be victims of trafficking:[2]

- Unusually tired during the day, sleeping during classes.

  Many of them are made to work long hours into the night despite also being required to attend school the next morning to avoid suspicion.

- Signs of physical abuse or neglect such as bruising or unkempt hair and clothing.

  Many victims are beaten by both johns and their pimps, leaving telltale bruises in places they cannot hide. They are not always given clean clothing or the chance to bathe. They may be too thin from food being withheld or not provided.

- Missing a lot of school, truancy.

  Victims are made to work despite being required to be at school, or they must stay home until obvious bruises or injuries heal.

- Bragging about money or flashing an unusual amount of money.

  *Victims are not always beaten. Some are gifted with lavish gifts or money in amounts that seem unusual for a child to have, in a behavior known as **grooming**.*

- Mental or emotional issues, acting out.

  Victims may suffer from both mental and emotional issues as they are unable to cope with what is happening to them. Some will act out in different ways, from misbehaving in order to draw attention to themselves, fecal smearing, disruptive behavior, and suicidal ideation.

- Severe guilt, depression, and anxiety.

Victims may feel guilty about the things they may be forced to do, or they may feel depressed or anxious because of the abuse.

- Substance abuse or Eating Disorders.

More severe coping mechanisms can follow if the victim is not given the proper interventions and the harmful behavior does not stop. Children may begin to abuse alcohol and drugs or may develop eating orders as a way to regain control over something in their lives.

- Self Harm.

Victims may begin to cut themselves in places that may not be visible to anyone else, or they may be reckless about the harm they cause to their body, leaving large scars on their arms, legs, and stomachs.

- Hypersexual Behavior.

Victims may present sexual behaviors at inappropriate times or inappropriate ages, sometimes acting out sexual behaviors on other children or adults.

At eighteen years old, Trixie had seen more of life's ups and downs than most people twice her age. Having been left in foster care at an age where she could just barely remember what her parents had looked like, she developed a terrible depression and dangerously rebellious nature that saw her in trouble more often than not.

She ran away from home often and was picked up for petty theft and shoplifting even more regularly than that. Her foster families traded her in and out for years, and she never truly had a sense of what it felt like to belong someplace.

Or someone.

Abuse and isolation were nothing new, and she looked forward to the day when she could be out on her own and live her life on her own terms. She knew it would be tough to get a start on her own, so she made sure to begin preparing long before her eighteenth birthday.

She already had two full-time jobs from the day she had graduated high school, and when her birthday finally came a month later and she was unceremoniously kicked out on her own, she was ready with a studio apartment lease and second-hand furniture that same morning.

Her age meant that she had finally aged out of the foster system that had done the bare minimum to help raise her, or at least look like it on paper, and she was finally responsible for raising herself. Trixie soon realized that it meant a life of shuttling between three dead-end jobs that barely covered the bills, only to spend what little free time she had sitting in a depressingly sparse box of an apartment that she paid for too much for anyway.

Welcome to Las Vegas: the City of Sin and hidden poverty.

She was a waitress, a rideshare driver, and by night she donned the classic Vegas feathers and glittering bikini to walk the strip and convince strangers to take photographs with her at ridiculous prices.

Partying in Vegas was a must, and she found herself in so many sketchy places over the first few months she moved to the city that she worried she'd end up in a ditch somewhere if she didn't keep track of her surroundings.

One night, all of that changed, and Trixie thought she had found herself a prince among the party-goers by the name of Lucas. He was charming and he was fast, but Trixie found herself swirled up in his world as quickly as he had laid eyes on her.

Little did she know how dangerous of a world it really was.

Lucas had helped Trixie to develop the little sense of self-worth and value that she had, and she felt she owed him a debt she could never truly repay. He lauded her with gifts and praise, and soon she realized that his kindness was a façade he had used to draw her in like a fly to honey.

Of course, there had been red flags, but she was too far gone in love to care about his endless string of phone calls and mysterious texts that had him leaving their shared apartment at all hours of the day and night.

"Why do you have to leave now? It's 2:30 on a Tuesday, Lucas!"

She was pissed, and he ignored her as usual as he got dressed and put on his shoes after the second phone call he had received in less than an hour. She had no idea where he was going, or who he was going to be with, but Lucas quickly made it clear that she wasn't to question him.

"Mind your fucking business Trixie, or I'll kick you out on that street and have another little bitch in your place so fast she'll be wearing your clothes. I do what I want when I want. If you question me again, I'll make sure you regret it."

Though his personality could be rough at times, Lucas provided life for her, he was kind to her for the most part, and he made love to her like she was the only person in the world.

She thought that she could live with his secrets if it meant not having to say hello to abject loneliness ever again. Lucas began to change even more, and the changes began to frighten her. He would no longer let her leave the house if she wasn't by her side. He began to bring strange men to their apartment at all hours without any real reason or explanation.

She never liked the way they looked at her like she was a piece of meat for the taking or cattle on display. They touched her without her permission, and Lucas never did anything to stop it.

"Why don't you ever say anything to your friends about putting their hands on me?"

Lucas shrugged and ignored her as she stood in front of the TV and blocked his view. She was dancing on thin ice, and she knew it was only a matter of time before he got angry.

"They do what they want to do. They are my friends. My things are their things. You're my thing, aren't you Trixie? How about you shut up and be happy that someone besides me can even put up with you."

When the abuse started, she had no one to turn to. Lucas had made sure to isolate and separate her from the few friends she had made over the years, and when his kindness dissolved into a monstrously controlling personality, Trixie realized that she was all alone in a world she knew nothing about.

"They don't give a shit about you, Trixie. They've been jealous of you from the moment they met you. Just forget them already. You have me. That's more than enough, isn't it?"

This is a typical tactic used by abusers:[2] making the victim feel alone and unwanted by others who could possibly help them. They work to isolate the victim and make them feel like they have no one else in the world to turn to but the perpetrator of the abuse.

She felt guilty at having doubted him, despite the newly forming bruise on her left cheek. He always gave her everything she needed. It was greedy to ask for more.

When Lucas began to spend time with younger and younger women, Trixie tried her hardest not to think about it.

She had finally reached a point in her life where she had someone who loved her.

Who cared if he loved someone else? Who cared if there were more than one, and they were far too young for her to even want to think about?

Her own home had become something foreign to her, and Lucas began to bring his friends back home after their long nights of doing God knows what out in the streets. They always had a girl or two in tow, and Trixie was warned not to disturb them, no matter what she heard.

It was early on a Tuesday morning that she realized exactly what that meant when she had been woken from her sleep by screaming that had suddenly stopped.

When she went to the kitchen to get a glass of water and shake the sleep from her head, she noticed a young girl standing in the bathroom at the end of the hall. She was wearing nothing more than a tattered and torn t-shirt, and there was blood dripping down from between her legs. She noticed Trixie after a moment and walked towards her on unsteady legs.

It was clear the girl had been drugged.

"Hi, miss, could you help me? I don't know where I am and I have school in a few hours and..."

"Hey! Get back here!"

Lucas shouted at the girl from down the hall, and Trixie cowered at the sound in his voice.

She knew that tone. Someone was going to end up bleeding that night, and for the first time in a long time, it wasn't going to be her.

"Please, Miss."

The girl looked afraid. She couldn't have been more than sixteen years old, but Trixie didn't do a thing to stop Lucas as he came down the hall and dragged her back to the room filled with his friends.

Red Flags, all of them.

Trixie didn't let it stop her from seeking Lucas' warmth when he finally came to bed that night. It didn't matter that he smelled like another woman, a woman who had not wanted to be there to begin with. She tried not to think of the ones who came before. She tried not to think of the ones who would come after.

She pushed the memory down and away with so many others she had discarded over her life.

It was the only way she had been able to survive.

When she woke in the middle of the night, the party had moved into their bedroom.

This time, however, Trixie was the prize.

She supposed the heroin they shot her up with made it all easier to bear, as she couldn't remember anything the next morning. The only things she had to remind herself of what happened were the bruises and the constant ache between her legs. When she brought it up with Lucas days later, she was met with a quick backhand across the face that left her lower lip swollen and bleeding.

"You made me a lot of money that night, Trixie, and I have no mind to stop. We have to keep this roof over our head somehow, right? Think of it as finally doing your part."

He was so good at making her feel guilty for all the love he gave her that no one else had ever bothered to. She was starting to wonder if it was worth it, but the idea of leaving left knots in her stomach made her feel sick. Where would she go? Who would she turn to? She didn't have a penny to her name. Everything she needed to survive came from Lucas.

A city like Las Vegas would swallow up a teen like her whole and spit her out in pieces. She couldn't afford to be alone. He was all she had.

Trixie began to get thin on account of the drugs and the eating disorder she had developed almost overnight. Her youthful curves melted away into hard angles and sharp protrusions, and her once bright eyes were now dull and lifeless.

"You need to keep yourself together. I can't get half the money I used to for you. Eat, goddamn it."

Binging soon became Trixie's only real friend, and between days at the bar and nights in random men's beds, she hardly recognized herself anymore.

The only constant in her life was Lucas, and even he had changed into something unrecognizable.

He didn't even try to hide the other women anymore. They lived right under the same roof as her and Lucas.

The day Trixie finally found the courage to run away was the most terrifying day of her life.

Lucas had kept her from saving any money or contacts from her past, and he was also keeping close tabs on her between the clients he forced her to take during the day as well. She quit her job at the bar, but she had hidden away enough tips that she could get to the East coast and have some money left over to find a place to stay and get a fresh start.

Though he did not come looking for her, Trixie lived in the shadows of her past as she tried to rebuild her life. Her eating disorder began to take its toll, and her weight fluctuated so drastically that friends at work started to take notice.

Though she had escaped her past, she had been left with scars and trauma that would take a lifetime to heal from. Trixie always kept her head on a swivel, knowing that the day would come when Lucas would come sauntering back into her life, filled with promises and love that she now knew was a ruse to get lonely young women to trust men like him.

For Trixie, she had escaped her situation but still faced a long road ahead in order to heal. There were stages to this healing that she would have to go through, the first of which being the **Victim/Outcast Stage**[4a]. In this stage, Trixie must recognize that she was a victim and let go of the guilt associated with her past circumstances.

The next stage is the **Survivor Stage**[4b] in which the victim tries to move on from the abuse, seeking help and therapy and a network of individuals to help them through. Trixie must recognize that something bad happened to her, but she survived, and the next step was up to her.

The next Stage is the **Thriving Stage**[4c], in which the victim is no longer merely just getting by, but making progress in their everyday life. Healing is taking place, and progress is constant. In this stage, Trixie must allow herself to love life again by making friends, finding hobbies, and planning for the future.

The final Stage is the **Victor/Leader Stage**[4d] in which the former victim has finally defeated their past and has gone beyond thriving into leading overs to thrive as well. Trixie must use her journey in order to help others find their path as well.

Trixie had been trying and failing, to move on from her past with Lucas for months, but despite the fact that he was no longer controlling her life, she felt as if she herself had lost control.

Work was easy enough, and unlike life in the big city, she had been able to scrape by on one full-time job instead of three. More free time meant more time to think, and Trixie hated remembering her past so much that she tried hard to regain some of that control she had lost. The sexual assaults had stopped, but the hardest part had now begun.

Trixie had to find a way to heal.

She wasn't able to bring herself to date just yet, and making friends was difficult but thankfully not impossible due to her job as a barista at a trendy café downtown.

Mental issues had already begun to plague Trixie when she first went into foster care, but it became much worse with the abuse she suffered at the hands of her boyfriend and the men who paid him to allow them to hurt her.

She had suffered from sleepless nights, anxiety, depression and self-harm while she had been trafficked, but even after escaping that life, the mental issues did not stop.

She began to have anger issues, lashing out at the kindest of people in her life without warning. She always felt incredibly guilty afterward, and soon the guilt ate away at her constantly. Trixie went as far as to blame herself for all she had been through, despite knowing deep down that she had not been the one to at fault.

Many victims of **Trafficking suffer from Mental Health issues**[5] during and after their ordeal. Some signs of mental issues present as follows:

- Sleeplessness and Nightmares.

  Victims may have trouble sleeping due to recurring nightmares or ingrained fear of being harmed while asleep.

- Anxiety.

  Victims may suffer from severe anxiety that interferes with their ability to function.

- Depression.

  Victims may suffer from depression brought on by the trauma they endure and the hopelessness of their situation.

- Low Self Esteem/Self Worth

  Victims may feel as if they have no worth due to the constant abuse and mistreatment they face.

- PTSD

  Victims may suffer from PTSD, which manifests in many different ways and can affect every aspect of their daily lives.

The best way for these victims to seek help is through a therapist or program that deals with sexual assault and trauma, following the SAMSHA approach to trauma care:

SAMSHA[6] recognizes the four R's as being essential in treating trauma patients.

- Realization about trauma and how it affects people.

- Recognizing the signs of trauma.

- Response to trauma that is appropriate and informed.

- Resisting re-traumatization.

For Trixie to receive the best care and therapy, she should seek a provider or facility that operates based on the SAMSHA approach to trauma care. She also has several different ways in which she can seek support for her recovery through

- Family and Friend Support.

  Trixie should surround herself with people who care for her and support her best interests, as well as those who can be there to listen when she needs an ear.

- Professional Support

  Trixie should seek Professional help through a licensed therapist or facility.

- Faith-Based Help

  Trixie can also find support through Faith-based programs.

Another way in which Trixie's mental health issues manifested was in her eating habits.

Eating had always been strictly controlled by the people in her life, from cruel foster families that withheld it, to Lucas who used it to torture her by either overfeeding or underfeeding her for days on end.

Now it was Trixie's turn to control how much she ate and when she ate it, and she found that she felt more in control when she was restricted than when she didn't.

Her thinness was alluring at first, and she quickly caught the attention of many of the men who regularly stopped at the café before work or on their lunch break. Trixie's fear of her history with Lucas repeating itself always brought her spiraling back down when she met someone with a nice smile or who brought butterflies to her stomach.

"You should take him up on his offer, Trixie, and go out sometime. He seems nice enough."

Her coworker, Michelle, an older woman who had tried and failed to take Trixie under her wing after sensing her need for someone positive in her life, tried to help her out of her shell every chance she could.

"He's really cute. You should try to be nicer to him next time. He seems to like you. A lot of people do, Trixie."

She was referring to one of their regular customers who stopped in for a large black coffee every morning. He had told her his name was Jason. She told him she hadn't asked.

Trixie sighed and tried to ignore the woman's kind smile, but was drawn in by her pleasant and welcoming demeanor. She was the only one she worked with who hadn't mentioned her weight, nor the scar patterns from the cutting on her upper arms.

"How about you come and join me for dinner instead one night? We can stop by my church first and take in the service if you'd like."

Trixie didn't like the sound of any of it, but the thought of not having to spend another night alone eating microwaved dinner was too good to pass up.

"Alright, Michelle, but it's just a one-time thing. I don't really have the time for new people in my life. I'm not really a church person either. I'm not sure if I believe in all of that."

Michelle nodded but remained open and friendly.

"He believes in you, Trixie. It might be a nice change of pace at any rate. You can meet some new people since you don't seem to like the ones at the café."

Trixie smiled and shrugged.

"Jason seems nice enough, it's just...hard to trust people."

Hard to trust men, especially.

The truth was, Trixie didn't have anyone in her life and she craved Michelle's friendship like a thirsty man in the desert craved water, she just didn't want to come off as too desperate.

It turns out the dinner Michelle was referring to was a homemade meal with her family, and as Trixie sat amongst Michelle's three children and aging husband, she felt completely out of place.

She didn't know how to act in a family setting. She had never had one of her own.

The dinner was thankfully light enough that Trixie felt safe in nibbling on more than half of the meal that was set in front of her, and she could see the relief in Michelle's eyes as she enjoyed her meal.

Michelle luckily caught wind of her discomfort and cut the meal short, allowing Trixie to go outside and stretch her legs.

Eating Disorders as a Manifestation of Sexual Trauma[7]

For some survivors of sexual trauma, eating issues develop as both a way to punish themselves further for what has happened to them, or to seek an aspect of control over something in their life.

It may begin while they are being trafficked, when pimps would withhold food and meals as punishment, forcing the victim to depend on another completely for meals and sustenance. Breaking free of this life, the victim may choose to continue to restrict food as a way of regaining control over that aspect of their lives.

For some, it may be a way for them to be able to control something in their lives when they feel powerless about everything else.

As Trixie walked along the street in Michelle's suburban neighborhood, she wondered why she had never been blessed with a life like that. The houses were large and the lawns were immaculate and the neighbors all waved at her despite never seeing her before in their lives.

Something about the welcoming nature of it all made her feel more alone than ever. She was tired of being alone.

She wished there was someone who always wanted to be by her side, but she knew no such person would or could ever exist.

Perhaps she was looking in the wrong place, and the night in church only served to fuel that notion inside of her head.

The service at Michelle's church was something Trixie had only ever seen on television, and it was nothing at all like she imagined. Everyone was welcoming to her, but it was only after she heard the story of Christ and everything he did for the world that it started to grab her interest.

"Why would someone do that? Why would they suffer so badly just so other people wouldn't have to?"

Michelle explained everything she knew about Christ to Trixie, and from that moment on she was intrigued, but not enough to regularly take part in the church.

The two became careful friends, but Michelle was unable to convince Trixie to join her at church again. She did, however, agree to meet up with the man from the bookstore who had been eyeing her. He seemed harmless enough, and a date at the café after her shift seem safe despite knowing that no one else would be there once she closed down.

Jason arrived thirty minutes after her shift ended, and she unlocked the doors of the café to let him inside while she finished closing down.

At first, he was the perfect gentleman, and they shared stories while sipping coffee and watching the rain begin to fall outside. It was romantic and perfect, and for the first time in a long time, Trixie began to feel hope.

An hour later and Jason bid her goodnight, with the promise to meet her again the next night after they closed down. She quickly obliged and the following evening couldn't come fast enough.

Even Michelle noted her enthusiasm, giving her a wink when Jason came in that morning to grab his usual coffee and left with a 'see you tonight,' that couldn't be mistaken for anything else.

That night, she closed up alone and Jason came at the appointed time. Just like the night before, they talked and shared coffee, but when it came time to leave, everything changed.

Trixie went to the back to close up the office and turn off the lights, but as she reached for the switch, she felt Jason's hand close over hers and turn off the light for her.

She move away from him quickly, but she couldn't see where she was going in the dark back room.

"Jason? What are you doing? Cut the light back on until I can clear the path."

She knew where the exit was, and she decided not to play any games and get out of there as quickly as she could.

"I didn't say you could leave, did I?"

Jason's voice had changed into something more commanding and less patient, and Trixie was scared.

"Come here, Trixie. How about you and I cut the nonsense and really get to know each other? You seem like the easy enough type, so let's not make this any more difficult than it has to be. Besides, you invited me here willingly, and there won't be a person alive who didn't know what you wanted when you did that."

When his hands closed around her mouth and wrist simultaneously, she knew what would happen next, as she had been left in this position many times before by Lucas. The men always got what they wanted. She was never strong enough to fight them off.

In the aftermath, Trixie felt dirty and used. She struggled to dress as he quickly put his clothes back on and made for the door. He looked down at her and sneered as he spoke, making her feel even worse than before.

"No one will believe you anyway. They'll all say you wanted it."

She couldn't take anymore, and Trixie began to scream as loud as she could, hoping to drown out his words. She screamed until he left, and that was the last time Trixie set foot in the café again. She left without notice or regard for anyone around her.

She left without cleaning up the blood stain on the floor in the back room, too ashamed to face what had happened to her in a place that had become her sanctuary.

Trixie tried to ignore it instead, allowing it to exacerbate her mental health issues until she was a shell of her former self.

She convinced herself she was better off alone, and she stopped trying to make connections with the people around her.

No one bothered to call her except for Michelle, and so she moved on from that first foray into adult life fairly quickly. She blocked Michelle's calls and continued to work and sleep, sleep and work, hoping for a way out of the desperation she still felt inside.

Her weight was beginning to become problematic, and her thinness was drawing concerned stares and questions from people who thought they were being helpful, sending Trixie into a depression every single time.

She got a job doing customer service online, that way she could avoid people and the public as much as possible.

She began to get everything delivered, avoiding the need to make trips to the store and being seen, and soon she could see her skeleton just beneath the thin layer of her skin.

She was lucky she didn't have anyone to worry about her, but her desired exile didn't stop her from having to leave the house now and then. Emerging one day to pick up necessities she couldn't get delivered, Trixie was shocked as she turned the aisle and nearly collided with a woman she instantly recognized.

"Trixie, is that you? It's me, Michelle, from the café! Oh, honey, you look a fright. Let's get you something to eat first thing, alright?"

She knew her thinness was shocking, but she didn't care. She was finally in control of something in her life. It was the only thing in the world that made the pain stop, even for a moment.

Michelle led her to the closest restaurant and told her to order anything she wanted, but Trixie hadn't eaten a real meal in so long that she couldn't decide. Michelle decided for her, and after the first few bites, Trixie was making a trip to the bathroom that didn't go unnoticed by her former coworker.

When she reemerged, Michelle looked at her with concern in her eyes. Trixie was far too thin, and her clothes hung off of her body like moss on an old oak tree. Her hair was thin and stringy, and her eyes had bags under them that were as dark as night. She wasn't taking care of herself, and it was evident to anyone who set eyes on her.

"Trixie, sweetheart. I can see that you're going through some terrible things in your life, and I want you to know that you aren't alone. He is always with you. Why don't you take a second look at the church I belong to and see if it's a good fit for you? There are other ways to control your life than with your weight, my dear."

Trixie felt shame at Michelle's words, but she also felt a sliver of hope. What could it hurt to give it another try?

She attended church with Michelle that week, and the following week after that. She stayed quiet the entire time, simply soaking in the message and the atmosphere. No one pushed her, but they remained friendly and open, and she began going to church weekly with Michelle, transforming her life one message of hope at a time.

Jason found her number and began to call incessantly. It was one of the methods he had used to stalk her after she had disappeared from the café without letting him know where she had gone.

As if he didn't know she was trying to get away from him.

She never picked up, but it didn't stop him from repeating the same harassing behavior night after night for weeks on end. Trixie eventually changed her number, but she worried that she might run into him in a town that wasn't as large as she had hoped.

It was a long journey that didn't happen overnight, as Trixie still had her doubts and had trouble trusting people and letting them close. Her eating disorder was in remission within six months, and Trixie was holding down a regular job at another café and meeting with Michelle and her group of friends outside of the church as well.

It became clear early on that Trixie had not been leading a Christian life, and it was time to make the necessary changes in order to find the peace she was still looking for.

She began to pray daily and attend service three times a week. She began to be more giving and tithe freely and participate in the community the church offered her.

She felt safe and welcome, and for the first time in her life, Trixie knew what it felt like to have a family.

She still had her past to contend with, unfortunately, and just as she began to make changes in her life, someone showed up that she wasn't yet ready to face.

Lucas.

"There you are, my beautiful Trixie. I've been looking everywhere for you, girly. Come over here and give me a kiss, why don't you? For old time's sake?"

Trixie's blood ran cold as soon as she heard the voice, she knew that Lucas had found her and her fight or flight instincts kicked into high gear.

Before he could get a chance to speak again, Trixie bolted out the back door and through the alleyways behind the row of businesses that sat just off of the highway, desperate to escape him.

She could see a crowd up ahead, and she thought she had a chance to be free of him and the threat he represented, but as she approached and called out to them, the one person who turned to face her was another face she would have rather not ever seen again: Jason.

He smiled at her and she stopped in her tracks, looking back towards where Lucas approached. Lucas looked every bit as dangerous as he actually was, and Trixie saw a chance to make sure that Jason never bothered her again.

She turned around and allowed Lucas to catch up to her and take her into his arms, his tattoo-covered arms and teardrop-covered cheeks a clear message to anyone to stay away.

She allowed Lucas to lead her away, and when she looked back, Jason was no longer looking in her direction.

"Would you like to go to church with me tonight, Lucas?"

She was trying to distract him, anything to keep him from taking her away from the new life she had built for herself.

He grimaced and spat on the sidewalk next to his beat-up truck, and Trixie wanted to be anywhere other than there with him. She didn't know what to do or where to turn, but in the back of her mind she had one new weapon she never had before:

Her faith.

"I can't miss church, Lucas. I go three times a week now. You should join me and you can even help me prepare a dish for the picnic this weekend.

"I'm not taking part in any of that nonsense, Trixie. You're gonna get in this car right now, is what you're gonna do, and we're going home. You've had enough time running around on your own. It's time I reminded you who you belong to."

Trixie couldn't see a way out that didn't end in violence other than getting in the truck with Lucas and letting him have his way with her, but something powerful was on her side, and she kept faith that she would be alright.

"Trixie? Trixie, is everything okay?"

In the nick of time, Michelle and her bible study group emerged from the restaurant next door and spotted Trixie in her predicament immediately. Had she decided to go with them and take the later shift, she would have missed running into Lucas altogether.

She couldn't dwell on that now, however, and she rushed around Lucas to stand near Michelle and the group of men and women who accompanied her.

Lucas was at a loss, as it was clear that Trixie had a different life now and she was no longer alone. She would no longer be easy to isolate or hurt without other people knowing.

"Forget you, I wish I never met you!"

With that, Lucas drove out of her life for what he thought was the last time. Trixie knew that other girls were still in danger and she wasn't going to let him, or Jason, get off with what they did to her so easily.

She turned to Michelle and embraced the woman with a grateful smile, and the two walked together and talked as her group continued on without her.

"If you don't mind me prying, who was that?"

They sat together on a bench overlooking the local park, and Trixie wrung her hands together in her lap as she tried to figure out what to say.

"He was an ex-boyfriend who turned abusive, so I took everything I owned in the middle of the night a year ago and ran away from him. I don't even know how he found me, but I can't go back to that life. I would have thought I had already aged out anyway."

Michelle frowned, not understanding her meaning.

"Aged out of his prostitution ring. Got too old to bring in the good money. I'm only nineteen now, but he started me early. I didn't have anyone to turn to or ask for advice on account of being a foster, so it was bad for a while until I got out."

Michelle finally realized that they had been talking about human trafficking, and her heart ached for Trixie.

"I'm so sorry. The church has a group for sexual assault survivors, Trixie, and I'm sure they could help you through this if you'll give them a chance. There is something else. The night that you quit at the café and never came back, you had a date with that Jason guy, right?"

Trixie swallowed hard and nodded.

"When I was cleaning up the back room the next morning, I found blood on the floor and a used bloody condom tossed behind the merch stacks. I thought the two of you had just gotten really frisky, but if something else happened, you should tell someone."

Trixie felt her heart race in her chest, knowing that Michelle was right, but not possessing the strength to face her abusers head-on in order to make them pay.

"Jason wasn't exactly the nice guy we thought he was, and he decided he wanted something I wasn't willing to give. He took it anyway."

Michelle paled and opened her arms for Trixie to hug her if she wanted, worried about initiating unwanted physical contact after all she had been through.

"Come to church with me tonight, Trixie. It will help get a load off of your chest."

Trixie enjoyed the service yet again, and afterward, Michelle introduced her to the rape counselor they had on staff.

She encouraged Trixie to go to the police on account of both men, but she couldn't see herself doing that. She was afraid of retaliation and worse, she was afraid no one would believe her.

"He believes you. He believes in you. Think of how many other young women you could save."

Trixie knew that she was right. If she wanted to dedicate her life to Christ, she had to learn to do the right thing, and the right thing was making sure no one else got hurt because she didn't speak up. She thought of Christ and of his journey and his sacrifice. She thought that his choice had been the right choice.

Telling the truth and helping to protect others was part of her Christian duty, and she wanted nothing more than to make Him proud.

She made arrangements to meet with detectives and to give what evidence she could to the police on her assault at the café, but it was Michelle who was the real life-saver.

"You know they have surveillance cameras back there, and likely have video evidence of everything that happened that night."

As luck would have it, the owner was able to provide the evidence she needed, and even with nothing more than a first name, Jason wasn't hard to track down. He worked with at-risk youth at the local shelter, and she felt as if she had saved more vulnerable women just like her than she would ever know.

Throughout the trial, Trixie relied on her newfound faith to see her through the hardest parts, and her new friends from church were there to support her every step of the way.

She only hoped Lucas would go down just as easily, but it was Lucas himself who was responsible for his downfall, Trixie just helped to put the nail in the coffin with her testimony.

He was caught transporting young girls across the border of Mexico and into Texas in order to service clients but was caught before he could deliver them. Lucas was off the street, and the lives of twelve girls were changed overnight.

Trixie was one of them.

The hardest part of Trixie's battle was over, but now the healing had to begin. She had seen the power of faith and how it had gotten her through the darkest parts of her life, and she didn't want to ever let it go.

Trixie was determined to heal, and she was determined to live her life to the best of her ability from that moment on.

She began to see a therapist with help from the church counselor, and she was thriving in the healing that came with being able to reveal everything she had gone through.

Trixie also had the healing power of Christ on her side, and she was ready to give back to the community that had given her so much.

Trixie began teaching a nonprofit class teaching vulnerable populations how to spot dangerous situations, and how to escape abusive relationships before the abuse becomes more widespread.

Her words traveled far and wide, and she was able to counsel many girls and young women who were at risk and in unhealthy relationships away from the danger that they were in.

She had big plans for dismantling the world of human trafficking, but she knew she had to start small.

It wasn't a matter of if, however, but only a matter of when for Trixie knew she could do anything with the power of faith and with her belief in Christ.

Faith-based healing and help may not be the right path for every victim of sexual trafficking. As it is with Susan, she needs to seek the main approach of Therapy and Professional Help, as well as building a strong support system that can prevent a recurrence of the trauma.

Mirabelle, the eldest of the two trafficked sisters, finally found herself free of her pimp, but without a support system in place, she quickly fell to life in the streets, falling into the same life she had just escaped from in order to fuel her heroin habit and to have a place to sleep.

Not everyone finds success when trying to turn their life around for the first time, but with the availability of outreach programs and help for trafficking victims, there is always hope.

Mirabelle eventually found herself at a halfway house that allowed her to finally be free of the life that she had tried so hard to escape. She sought treatment for her drug addiction first, then her trauma soon after, hoping to break the cycle she had been caught in since she was a little girl. The progress was slow at first, but she kept at it, and soon she was finding the successes in life that she had once only dreamed of.

Her first apartment was followed by her first cat, and a boyfriend who was patient and understanding fell into place soon after. She was making friends and building a support system.

Mirabelle was finally thriving. She sought therapy for her trauma and her survivor's guilt after discovering the fate of her sister. She was able to bring the once unclaimed remains of Eliza home and give her a proper burial like she deserved.

Mirabelle sought care from a SAMSHA trauma informed therapist who made sure that she provided an environment for her to get better. Her Therapist made sure to follow the Trauma-informed Care Principles that made her feel like she made the right choice.

Trauma-informed Care Principles

- Safety

  The environment for care must be safe from anything or anyone that can cause harm.

- Trustworthiness

  The provider must be open and trustworthy in order to make the patient feel at ease.

- Peer Support

  The provider must utilize the guidance of others who have been in similar situations as the patient.

- Collaboration

  The provider must work with the patient and other doctors for the best care.

- Empowerment

  The provider must give the patient the power to make choices about the patient's care.

- Cultural Issues

The provider must be informed and sensitive to the issues that face different cultures, genders, or sexes.

Mirabelle now works at a halfway house providing counseling for at-risk youth and victims of trafficking. She founded a non-profit organization in honor of her sister that helps provide victims with a safe transition from being trafficked, to being safe. Mirabelle is now a leader, and she has broken the ties of addiction and the cycle of trafficking for good.

Trixie continued to counsel women and girls, and to provide classes for foster children to spot the signs of abuse and to give them resources for help.

Not every story has a perfect ending, but for some who escape trafficking, it is vital that they find support and therapy in order to live a fulfilling life free of the recurrence of trauma. It is also important that they and those in their lives recognize the stages of healing, signs of trauma or PTSD, signs of eating disorders and other mental health issues that a victim of trafficking might suffer from.

Police are available to help. There are runaway hotlines to call. There are safe houses available. There is a way out.

If you or anyone you know are a victim of trafficking, call

RUNAWAY/ TRAFFICKING HOTLINE

1-888-373-7888

Or just call 911 giving your location and name

~ ~ ~

For Suicidal Ideations and Suicide Prevention

LIFELINE/ HOTLINE

1-800-273-8255

For Suicide & Crisis, call the National Hotline,

988

For mental health/ substance abuse for emergency help, call,

1-800-662-4357

ENDNOTES

[1] **Topic:** Child Sex Trafficking, **Site:** Childrensrights.org

[2] **Topic:** Signs to look out for in children that maybe victims of trafficking, **Site:** Humantraffickingelearning.com

[3] Psychology Today article written by Lisa Aronson Fontes Ph.D, Invisible Chains, The Mind Control Tactics of Domestic Abusers (*May 27, 2021*).

[4a] **Victim/Outcast Stage**

[4b] **Survivor Stage**

[4c] **Thriving Stage**

[4d] **Victor/Leader Stage**

Topic: understanding the four stages of sex trafficking, **Site:** Humantraffickingelearning.com

[5] Mental health Resources for Human Trafficking Survivors and Allies, Catherine Chon, Director, Office of Trafficking in Persons, October 21,2021

[6] Implementing a Trauma – Informed Approach, Office to monitor and combat trafficking in persons, www. state.gov/j/tip, Washington, DC, June2018

[7] The Connection Between Eating Disorders and Sexual Violence, Laura Palumbo, February 25,2022, NSVRC (National Sexual Violence Resource Center), nsvrc.org

Smile

Jesus Loves

You

And

So do I